MW01106860

By Apple Jordan
Illustrated by Alex Maher

First published by Parragon in 2012
Parragon
Queen Street House
4 Queen Street
Bath BA1 1HE, UK
www.parragon.com

ISBN 978-1-4454-4753-7

Printed in China

Disney · PIXAR
TOY STORY

Backpack Adventure

A little story for little learners

Bath · New York · Singapore · Hong Kong · Cologne · Delhi
Melbourne · Amsterdam · Johannesburg · Auckland · Shenzhen

Andy could not
wait for school.
Today was
space day!

"I will bring my space ranger, Buzz Lightyear," he said.

Buzz was excited.
He loved
space day!

In class,
Andy learned
about space.

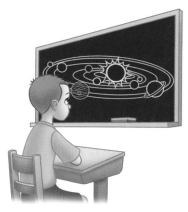

He learned
about the
stars and the
moon.

He learned
about the
sun and the
planets.

Brring!
The bell rang.
Lunchtime!

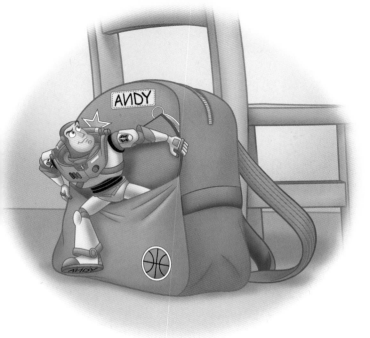

Buzz hopped out
of Andy's backpack.
He was ready
for fun!

Buzz saw
a hamster.
"Greetings,
strange creature,"
he said.

Buzz lifted the
lid to get a
closer look.

Uh-oh!
The hamster
jumped out.
It ran off.

"Come back!"

Buzz cried.

"I mean you no harm."

Oops!
Buzz fell into
a jar of paint.

SPACE
EXPLORATION

"Blast!" cried Buzz.
"I must clean
up and find
that creature."

Then Buzz met
some clay aliens.
He thought they
were space toys.

"Greetings,"
he said.
"Have you seen a
furry creature?"

They did not answer.
Buzz shook hands
with a space toy.
Its arm fell off.

"Sorry about that!"
Buzz cried.
He ran away.

Buzz landed on
a tower made
of blocks.

It wobbled
back and forth.
Crash!
At last it came
toppling down.

"All done!" said Buzz.

Then the bell rang.

The class came

back from lunch.

Buzz hopped
into Andy's backpack.
No one saw him.

The class got ready
for show-and-tell.
Andy went first.

"This is Buzz,"
he said.
"Buzz is the BEST
space ranger ever!"